Moon Mouse

Weekly Reader Children's Book Club *presents*

Moon Mouse

By Adelaide Holl

Illustrated by Cyndy Szekeres

Random House New York

Weekly Reader Children's Book Club Edition. Primary Division.

One evening, Mother Mouse
called to her baby.
"Come, Arthur," she said.
"Now that you are old enough,
you may stay up after dark.
Let us watch the night."

Arthur ran happily to the door
of the nest and looked out.
The black sky was all around him.
Darkness was everywhere.
The night was still and cool.
Arthur felt the coolness
on his little, pointed nose.
It touched his whiskers
and his round little ears.

"So this is what the night is like!"
he said happily. "It is lovely!"

Arthur looked up. There in the blackness
was something big and round and shining.
"Look!" he cried in excitement.
"Oh, look! Look!"
Mother Mouse smiled.
"It is only the moon," she said. "It is
the big, round, yellow moon."

13

"Where is the moon?" asked Arthur
with bright eyes.

"Very far away," his mother told him.
"Up, up, high in the sky."

"What is it for?" asked the little
mouse.

Mother Mouse said, "It shines
in the dark. It gives us light."

"What is it made of?"
asked Arthur in excitement.
"I do not know," answered
his mother. "I have heard
that it is made of cheese,
but I do not think so."

15

"I would like to go there,"
said Arthur. "I would like to go
to the moon."

His mother smiled. "Well, not tonight,"
she said. "Come, it is bedtime."

Arthur thought about the moon.
He thought about it day after day.
He thought about it night after night.

"How far away is the moon?"
he asked his mother one day.
"Very, very far," she told him.
"Farther than the edge of the meadow.
Farther than the farmer's cornfield.
Farther than the fields of golden wheat."

One evening, Arthur said to himself,
"I am old enough to stay up after dark.
I must be old enough to go to the moon."
    He looked up. The sky was dark
and misty. He could not see the round,
yellow moon anywhere.
    "I will go look for the moon,"
said Arthur to himself.
    So he set off all alone.

He went a long, long way—
past the edge of the meadow,
past the farmer's cornfield,
past the fields of golden wheat.

The sky was black and misty.
Then, little by little, the stars
began to come out.

Arthur went on and on
until he came to a place with many lights
and many noises.

And there, all at once, he saw the moon
sitting high on top of a tall building.

He looked about in great excitement.
He saw steps going up and up and up.

"This must be the way to the moon,"
he said. So he began to climb.

He climbed till he could go no higher.
And there he saw an open place
for going in.

"This must be the door to the moon,"
he said to himself. And in he went.

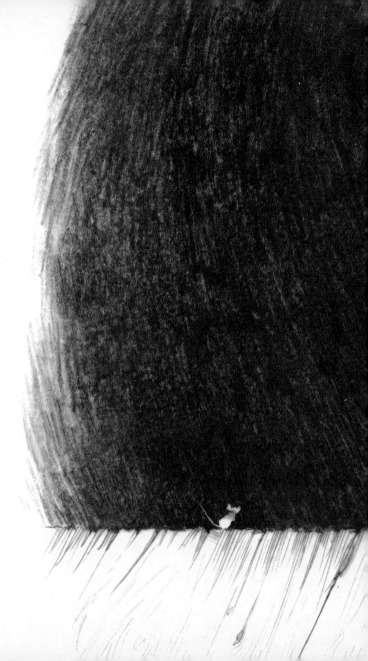

Sure enough! Inside was something
big and round and yellow. And it
was made of cheese!

"*It is the moon!*" cried Arthur,
his eyes big and shining.

He scampered all about. He ran
in and out of the little craters.
He nibbled a bit here.
He nibbled a bit there.
At last, he was very full
and very tired.

"The moon is a delicious place,"
he said to himself. "But I think
I shall go home now."

27

He
climbed
down,
all the way down,
to the ground.
    He went a long, long way—
past the fields of golden wheat,
past the farmer's cornfield,
past the edge of the meadow.
He went all the way home to his nest.

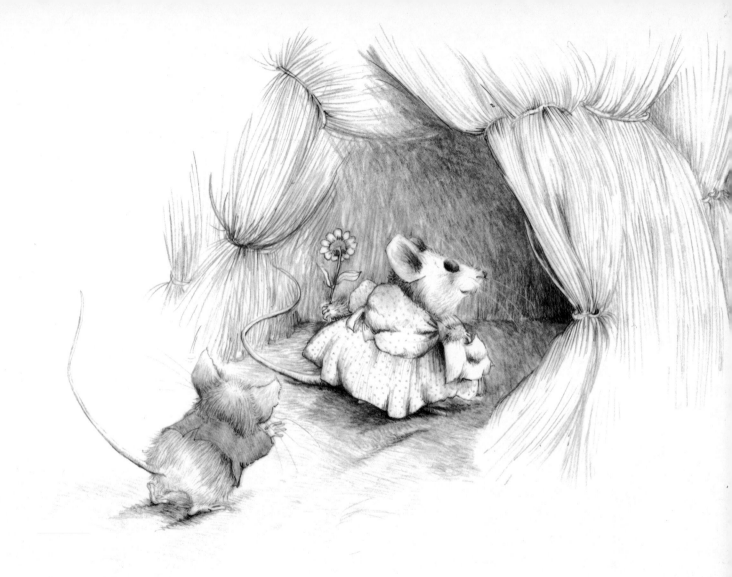

"Where on earth have you been?"
asked Mother Mouse. "I have been
looking for you."

"I have been all the way to the moon,"
said Arthur in excitement. "It *is* big, and
round, and yellow. It *is* made of cheese.
And it is very delicious!"

Mother Mouse smiled. "Funny little
mouse!" she said kindly.

Arthur looked up at the night sky.
A soft rain was falling. There was darkness
all about.

"Where is the moon?" he asked his mother.

"It is a rainy, cloudy night," she told
him. "The moon is hiding."

Arthur watched for the moon the next
night, and again the next. Night after night
he waited. But there was only the blackness
and the rain.

Then one evening, the rain stopped.
The clouds began to drift away.
All at once, the moon came out.
It was shiny. It was bright. But it was not
big and round. It was only a small, thin slice.
One whole side was missing.

"Look!" Arthur called to his mother in
excitement. "See what a lot of the moon
I nibbled!"

"So you did," said his mother with a smile.
"It is a good thing you did not eat it *all up!*"